DAREDEVIL SPORTS

BULL RIDING

By Hal Garrison

HOT TOPICS

Gareth Stevens
PUBLISHING

Please visit our website, www.garethstevens.com. For a free color catalog of all our high-quality books, call toll free 1-800-542-2595 or fax 1-877-542-2596.

Library of Congress Cataloging-in-Publication Data

Names: Garrison, Hal, author.
Title: Bull riding / Hal Garrison.
Description: New York : Gareth Stevens Publishing, [2018] | Series: Daredevil sports | Includes index.
Identifiers: LCCN 2017029988| ISBN 9781538211090 (pbk.) | ISBN 9781538211106 (6 pack) | ISBN 9781538211113 (library bound)
Subjects: LCSH: Bull riding--Juvenile literature.
Classification: LCC GV1834.45.B84 G37 2018 | DDC 791.84--dc23
LC record available at https://lccn.loc.gov/2017029988

Published in 2018 by
Gareth Stevens Publishing
111 East 14th Street, Suite 349
New York, NY 10003

Designer: Bethany Perl
Editor: Kate Mikoley

Photo credits: Cover, p. 1 Jim Parkin/Shutterstock.com; pp. 2-32 (background) Moran Ben-Herzel Kurt/Shutterstock.com; pp. 5, 21 Christopher Halloran/Shutterstock.com; pp. 7, 11, 17, 26 Kobby Dagan/Shutterstock.com; p. 8 Delmas Lehman/Shutterstock.com; p. 9 Dave Blackey/All Canada Photos/Getty Images; p. 10 photo-denver/Shutterstock.com; p. 13 Andrew Watson/Photolibrary/Getty Images; p. 15 Alison Scott/Corbis/Getty Images; p. 19 Pawel Papis/Shutterstock.com; p. 23 Chuck Szmurlo/Wikipedia.org; p. 25 alberto clemares exposito/Shutterstock.com; p. 27 Donald Miralle/Getty Images Sport/Getty Images; p. 29 Amcilrick/Wikipedia.org.

Printed in the United States of America

CPSIA compliance information: Batch #CW18GS: For further information contact Gareth Stevens, New York, New York at 1-800-542-2595.

CONTENTS

A RISKY 8 SECONDS

Sitting on top of a bull, the rider waits behind a gate. The crowd roars. The gate opens, and the bull charges into the **arena.** The rider only has to stay on for 8 seconds, but it's harder than you might think!

RISK FACTOR

Though it's over quickly, some people consider bull riding to be the most dangerous, or unsafe, 8 seconds in sports!

Bulls don't like being ridden. When a rider is on their back, they buck, or jump around, and try to throw them off. Staying on a bucking bull is hard enough, but riders are only allowed to hold on with one hand!

RISK FACTOR

Riders use one hand to hold onto a rope that's wrapped around the bull's chest. They usually keep their other hand up in the air.

FINALS

If a rider gets thrown off the bull or touches the ground before the 8 seconds are over, they get **disqualified**. They also get disqualified if their free hand touches their own body, the bull, or the rope during the 8 seconds.

RISK FACTOR

Bull riding often happens at rodeos. These are events where people take part in contests using horses, bulls, and other animals.

SCORING

Riders are scored for their skill. Bulls also get scored based on how hard they make the ride. The scores are added together, and the highest total score wins. If a rider gets disqualified, they don't get scored, but the bull still does!

RISK FACTOR

Each ride is worth up to 100 points, but scores above 90 are considered excellent!

GETTING READY

Before the ride, bulls are kept in a small, gated area called a chute. The rider gets on top of the bull there. This way, the bull doesn't have room to buck the rider off before the gate opens and the ride starts.

RISK FACTOR

Another rider often helps the rider prepare and get on the bull.

CHUTE

HOLD ON!

A bull-riding rope usually has a handle that's made partly of leather. This helps the rider hold on. Riders also wear spurs. These are pieces that attach to their boots and help the rider hold onto the bull with their feet.

RISK FACTOR

A weighted bell is attached to the rope under the bull's chest. This helps the rope fall off when the ride's over.

HANDLE

Being thrown from a bull is painful enough, but holding onto a rope while it's happening could cause a pretty bad rope burn. That's why riders wear a special **glove** on the hand they use to hold the rope.

RISK FACTOR

Riders often put **rosin** on the rope and glove. This makes the rope sticky and easier to hold onto.

GLOVE

SAFETY GEAR

Most riders wear special vests that help keep their bodies safe when they fall. These are made out of the same thing that is used to make **bulletproof** vests! Many riders also wear helmets and special gear to keep their legs safe.

RISK FACTOR

Bull riders are 10 times more likely to become seriously hurt than football players.

HELMET
VEST

A ROUGH LANDING

Once the 8 seconds are done, you might think the hard part is over. But the bull doesn't stop because the clock does. The rider still has to dismount, or get off the bull. Even skilled riders can get hurt dismounting.

RISK FACTOR

Falling off the bull is part of the sport. Knowing how to land in the safest possible way is one of the most important things a rider has to learn.

A & H

BULLFIGHTERS

After dismounting, riders need to get away from the bull as fast as possible. Once the rider hits the ground, the bull could try to hurt them. Bullfighters are people who keep the riders safe after they dismount.

RISK FACTOR

Bullfighters **distract** the bull so the rider has time to get up and get away from the bull.

TransCanada

RIDING HISTORY

Bull riding began in rodeos in the 1910s, though at first, a kind of bull called a steer was used. In the 1930s, chutes started being used in arenas, which allowed riders to use bulls like the ones used today.

RISK FACTOR

Today, bulls used for the event usually weigh between 1,700 pounds (770 kg) and 2,000 pounds (907 kg)!

In 1992, a group of bull riders who had taken part in the rodeo **circuit** came together. They formed a group called the Professional Bull Riders. Together, they made bull riding its own sport outside of rodeo.

RISK FACTOR

At the end of each season, one rider becomes the Professional Bull Riders world champion!

A DARING EVENT

Bull riding is an exciting, but dangerous, sport! It's often the most popular event at rodeos, and more than 300 professional bull riding events are held each year. People all over the world enjoy watching and taking part in this daring sport!

RISK FACTOR

Riders aren't the only popular ones in bull riding. Bulls that do well often become very well known with fans.

SAFETY TIPS

ALL BULL RIDERS SHOULD:

- exercise to stay strong and fit.
- wear proper safety vests, helmets, and other gear.
- practice with a skilled rider and learn the correct form.
- make sure the rope and bell are properly attached to the bull.
- learn how to properly dismount a bull.
- be able to quickly get away from the bull.

FOR MORE INFORMATION

BOOKS

Hamilton, John. *Bull Riding*. Minneapolis, MN: ABDO Publishing Co., 2014.

Hamilton, S. L. *Rodeo*. Edina, MN: ABDO Publishing Co., 2010.

WEBSITES

Eight Seconds of Bull Riding
www.kidzworld.com/article/6806-eight-seconds-of-bull-riding
Read more interesting information about this exciting sport here.

Riding Basics
www.pbr.com/en/education/riding_basics.aspx
Learn more about the basics of bull riding on the Professional Bull Riders website.

GLOSSARY

arena: an area or building where sports and other events take place

bulletproof: made to stop bullets, or small pieces of metal shot out of a gun

circuit: a series of events held at many different places

disqualify: to stop or prevent someone from being a part of something, usually for having broken a rule

distract: to cause something to stop paying attention to one thing and instead pay attention to something else

glove: a covering for the hand that has a part for each finger

rosin: a hard, sticky matter that has many uses

INDEX